http://www.camillamakesasplash.com

Copyright © 2024 Elizabeth Connell Lewis and Mark S. Lewis
Published in the United States by Story Leaders.
www.leaderspress.com

All rights reserved. No part of this book may be reproduced or transmitted in any form or by any means, electronic or mechanical, including photocopying, recording, or by an information storage and retrieval system – except by a reviewer who may quote brief passages in a review to be printed in a magazine or newspaper – without permission in writing from the publisher.
All trademarks, service marks, trade names, product names, and logos appearing in this publication are the property of their respective owners.

ISBN 978-1-63735-323-3 (hcv)
ISBN 978-1-63735-321-9 (pbk)
ISBN 978-1-63735-320-2 (ebook)

Library of Congress Control Number: 2024912769

Camilla
Learns to
Shine

Elizabeth Connell Lewis
and
Mark S. Lewis
Illustrator: Katya Kuznetsova

This book is dedicated to all
those who shine their light to
help others, especially Rebecca Guerra and
Kim Lewis James, who do so much
for our family.

"This little light of mine,
I'm gonna let it shine…"

- Gospel Hymn by Harry Dixon Loes

Nestled deep in the coral,
A place hard to find...
Lived a cuttlefish mother
And cuttlet most kind.

A baby cuttlefish is called a cuttlet.

Right after hatching,
Her siblings took leave,
But a small baby stayed
So her mom would not grieve.

Cuttlets hatch from eggs, which the mother cuttlefish places under rocks or coral to keep them safe from predators, such as sharks, seals, dolphins, and large fish.

This young mollusk daughter
Knew mom would be sad,
And by staying behind,
She would make Mama glad.

As soon as cuttlets hatch, they are ready to leave their mother and survive on their own, hunting small fish, shrimp, and crabs.

Mama watched closely
As cuttlet grew strong.
It became pretty clear, though,
That something was wrong.

For her young pretty daughter,
Flamboyant and bright,
Seemed ashamed of her arms
And her shape and her height.

Her squid cousins were larger
And graceful when swimming.
Their bodies weren't stubby
Their shapes were more slimming.

Flamboyant Cuttlefish are much smaller than other cuttlefish species. They grow to be only 6-8 cm in length. They are fatter than other cuttlefish and squid, with shorter arms and tentacles.

Embracing Camilla,
And holding her tight,
Mama insisted
Her shape was just right.

"You know, Mollusks can come
In all shapes and all sizes.
Some species swim better...
You're best with disguises."

Cuttlefish are mollusks and are related to squid, snails, octopuses, clams, oysters, and nautiluses.

"Your body," Mom said,
"Is designed best for crawling.
Most others can't do this
While they are out trawling."

Flamboyant Cuttlefish have a body that is specifically designed for crawling along the ocean floor.

"Camilla's a name that
Will set you apart.
It means, 'one who brightens
And warms others' hearts.'"

Flamboyant Cuttlefish can create their own light. This is called bioluminescence. They do this to warn predators, attract a mate or to mesmerize their prey.

"I hope you will do this
While making your way.
Your own special talents
Will brighten one's day."

Larger cuttlefish have larger cuttlebones and they are better swimmers than smaller cuttlefish.

Camilla began
To explore things outside...
By changing her texture
She could easily hide.

Cuttlefish are like chameleons. They can instantly change the color and texture of their body to hide from predators or sneak up on prey.

Specialized cells
Found all over her skin,
Helped her change colors
And quickly blend in.

Cuttlefish use special cells called chromatophores that allow them to change colors in seconds.

With her two tentacles
And her very keen eyes,
She could handily capture
Her food floating by.

Cuttlefish have excellent vision and can see in all directions, although they cannot see in color.

Cuttlefish, like their squid cousins, have a tubular shape called a mantle. They have 8 arms and 2 longer tentacles.

Hungry barnacles struggled,
Quite stuck in one spot.
Camilla fanned plankton
Their way to be caught.

As the sun sank down lower,
And darkened the sky,
Some starfish were struggling
To find food nearby.

Cuttlefish have unique eyes. Their pupils are shaped like the letter "W." Starfish have trouble seeing in dark water.

Camilla lit up,
Her light helped them see well.
The starfish were grateful...
This made her hearts swell!

A cuttlefish actually has three hearts!!

Camilla raced home
As fast as she could.
Quite eager to share...
And feeling so good!

Cuttlefish have a siphon that is used for jet propulsion. They can suck in water and shoot it out in any direction to help them move.

She crawled close to Mama,
And told of her actions...
How helping the others
Gave great satisfaction.

The mouth of a cuttlefish is located at the center of the 8 legs and is shaped like a bird's beak.

Both the tentacles and the arms are covered with suckers for gripping onto rocks and coral and for catching prey.

Mama just glowed,
Pulled Camilla in tight...
"Helping others feels good
With your fins and your light."

"You are such a bright girl,
And with so much to share...
Use your brain and your talents
To show that you care."

Cuttlefish have three brains, and they have one of the largest brain-to-body size ratios of any invertebrate (an animal without a backbone).

"Make a big splash and
Create your own waves.
Do the right thing
Every one of your days."

"Your ripples will spread...
They will reach near and far,
Making lives better
Wherever you are."

Notes to Readers:

In this book, Camilla Cuttlefish helps hungry barnacles by fanning plankton their way with her fins. She also helps struggling starfish by creating light in the darkening water so that they might better see the food they need. You can learn more about cuttlefish, barnacles, plankton, starfish, bioluminescence and more on our Make a Splash website by scanning the QR code below.

Camilla is learning that helping others, even in small ways, makes her feel good. How might you help others? For inspiration or to post your own ideas, go to www.CamillaMakesaSplash.com

Discussion and Questions to Consider

At the beginning of the story, Camilla chooses to stay with her mother, even though all her brothers and sisters leave. She doesn't want her mother to be lonely. Have you ever shared comfort and friendship with someone who was lonely or needed a friend?

Camilla doesn't like the way she looks in the beginning of the story. She wishes she had a larger and slimmer body and that she could swim better and faster. Her mother reassures her that her body is just right. Have you ever wished to look different or to have different abilities or skills?

Consider all the wonderful parts that make you unique and how you might use your special features and talents to help others.

About Elizabeth & Mark Lewis

Elizabeth Connell Lewis has been a teacher, writer, and gifted education specialist for over 30 years. Her passion is identifying and nurturing gifts and talents in children. *Camilla the Cuttlefish Learns to Shine* is her third children's book. To learn more about Elizabeth go to: www.CamillaMakesASplash.com.

Mark S. Lewis has been a successful leadership coach, author, professional speaker, and entrepreneur for over 30 years. His passion is helping adults, especially in the business world, realize how important it is to be caring, respectful, kind, empathetic and selfless (mlewis@marklewisllc.com).

Elizabeth and Mark are working together to encourage people of all ages to "make a splash" or do their part to make the world a better place. Look for their other Camilla "Makes a Splash" books!

A beautifully illustrated deep dive into the world—and hearts—of cuttlefish. This book is a gem for classrooms, libraries, and home bookshelves all the same.

Sara Gomez, Elementary School Librarian

This delightful book is overflowing with accurate and age-appropriate scientific information and engaging artwork. It is difficult to find children's story books that also contain interesting non-fiction information. As a parent, I believe the message of self-acceptance and appreciating one's unique talents is sorely needed in this day and age. I highly recommend this book for teachers' classrooms as well as home collections. Children will look back fondly on the book that "hooked" them to love and want to learn more about the wonders of marine life!

Sarah Root Pulliam, Marine Science Educator

Camilla Learns to Shine is a charming story that beautifully highlights the importance of embracing one's unique qualities. A delightful read that inspires confidence and celebrates diversity.

Alinka Rutkowska, USA Today and Wall Street Journal Bestselling Author

A delightful book that will be loved by all ages! The colorful artwork and science vocabulary make this book a winner!

Gina Watkiss, Elementary Science Specialist

This is a very kind story, and it can help you learn more about kindness and brightening up people's hearts, which might make your heart brighten up! I didn't know that cuttlefish brighten up with bioluminescence—like stars! You can be a bright star when you're kind!

Kora, a second-grade student

www.ingramcontent.com/pod-product-compliance
Lightning Source LLC
Chambersburg PA
CBHW041523070526
44585CB00002B/65